This craft I'm perfecting is dedicated to GOD first. Then my Moms, Grandma, son & G-son, 2 Aunts, All my Family And day ones, Can't forget my better half. Oh and All the Hustlers out here and the Hating ass sucker ass niggaz. & Love to the ones I forgot...

" A real hustler never gives up until they accomplish getting that bag By any means necessary."
Courtney "BLESS" Brown

The Lies We Live With

A Novel

by Bless

Table of Contents

Prologue

t's been a long week for Stacks. First, his plug dragged him into some bullshit, then his nephew started to jeopardize their paper. Stacks was just involved in a shoot-out that almost cost him everything. Right about now, Stacks needs a little time to unwind but he is too paranoid to stay in one spot. So, he pulls up to the back door of Richards Gentleman's Club and toots the horn. Seconds later, Tammy runs out. Tammy is a white chick, fine as a glass of wine carrying her Louis Vuitton clutch while sporting an all-white Ferragamo skirt, which stops just where the peak between her legs begins. Tammy jumps in and takes off her stilettos.

Just as Stacks pulls his Benz away from the curb, Tammy flips down the vanity mirror and applies a type of lip gloss appropriate for their night out together.

She looks at him with her sultry pout and says, "Stacks, I'm hungry for daddy's dick. Are you gon' let me have the little taste? Or can momma have the whole damn plate"

He smirks at her and says "Come here and tell me how this taste first, then maybe-just maybe you can move on to the full course." Tammy flashes another giggly smile, "Well let me see if it's cooked zaddy, and next time, don't go so long without feeding me."

Tammy reaches over the gear column and rubs through Stacks Givenchy Jeans, his dick raises to full attention. She unbuttons and unzips his denim then she reaches into his boxer briefs pulling out his rock-hard dick. "Is this all you called me from my job for?" Tammy asks while smiling at Stacks.

He cuts his eye at her while sending a smile at her. Stacks wheels the car down to Arthur Ashe

Blvd, as he drives down into Lakeside Ave, he figures choosing this route would be fewer whips in the traffic.

Tammy takes the tip of his head and wraps her lips around the most sensitive part of his pole, then pops it back out while blowing more cool air on it. The icy hot lip gloss she applied is starting to take effect like it's meant to. "Ooh shit Tammy, I swear... I would marry ya ass if I could." Stacks says with a gasp. "Well stop talking and do it then," Tammy says in between a juicy slurp! "Umm-Humm... Tammy, let me do the talking. You just eat." Stacks palms the crown of her head and eases himself deeper, this time tickling her tonsils. He then slides his index and middle fingers into her wet pussy from the back with ease; due to the fact, Tammy came out not wearing panties.

Stacks then trafficates left, turning into Bryant Park. It's after dark, so it will be perfect for him to give Tammy a biggie-sized combo meal in the back seat while parked overlooking the park's manmade lake. He drives about sixty yards into the park and sees a set of headlights through his rearview. Stacks pats the back of Tammy's head and she comes up for air. "What baby- You about to cum? Go ahead daddy, I won't spill a drop!" She says playfully.

Tammy bows her head attempting to go in for the kill, but Stacks stops her while saying to her, "Hell, naw boo, wait a minute for me." "What stacks?" "Some car pulled in back there, I couldn't tell if it was a cop or not, but on the safe side just hold tight til' we see who the fuck that is back there." "Okay babe," Tammy says while starting to get herself together.

Stacks quickly regroups and reacts to the circumstances, then real fast he hits a combination of controls on the dash, causing the stash spot to mechanically ajar, he keeps it open in case its twelve and they decide to fuck with him, and he has to throw his strap in it. Stacks then accelerates a little bit, allowing more distance between him and the vehicle behind him. Picking up speed on the narrow curvy lanes through the park. He allows the German engineering to assist him with the difficult task! "Fuck," Stacks yells out with the outburst. "Them motherfuckers seem like they are following us and got a nerve to be speeding up on us.... It doesn't look like a cop car, but looking at their headlights, it looks like a charger or something" "Just be calm baby," Tammy says while fixing her skirt and looking over her shoulder to see what Stacks was talking about.

Immediately Tammy had a straight shot at the view, she sees something Stacks couldn't. "Stacks, baby! It looks like all of them in that car got masks on!"

"You said what?" Stacks says as he hits a button on his touch screen and a rear-camera display pops up. "Fuck! That's the same niggaz that I got tha busting at the other day, I knew that charger looked familiar." "Stacks are you serious? What do you think they want?" "Bitch don't ask me no dumb shit, you know they ain't come to talk especially with fucking masks on. Look I'm gonna try to lose 'em real quick, then I will drop you off at the cut by the pond, I want you to get out and run and hide, and order yourself a uber soon as you think the coast is clear. When you get out, I will double back on them niggaz, park the car, and hide in the woods. When they spot my car and hopefully get out to examine it, I'm gonna hop out and let em' have it." "OK... Stacks! Don't forget I love you" "You don't love *me, gurl,* you just love my doggy style!"

He flashes a quick smile as he was leaning in for a peck on the lips, but inches away from what may be his last kiss, the driver behind them flashes their headlights and signals for him to pull over. Stacks floors it. The SUV gets up to about 75 in a 25-mph zone. He moves left around a corner, and seconds later, it's a sharp right, then he approaches a speed bump and glides right over it like it didn't even exist. According to the plan, he drove straight ahead, which took him to the pond. He peels a blue face hundred off the stack of money from the center of the console. He informed Tammy to dip from the car and text when she was safe. Tammy gets out and Stacks wheels the truck back into the direction he just came from. He gets back down the straightaway and veers around the first corner, then racks a bullet into the head of his 40 Cal. Glock, while contemplating where he's going to stop the truck and hide for the ambush.

Before he could make it to the second bend in the street where he planned to park to execute his ops, the driver of the charger pulls out of a bike path and cut into the woods and rams the back of the G-wagon sending the truck into a police-style pit maneuver. As Stacks tried to correct the wheel, the truck goes screeching sideways for about 15 feet and then flips over onto the passenger side making it skid six feet further. He lands upside down on his neck laying in the passenger area.

As he was mumbling something to himself about not wearing a seatbelt. He scrambled to find the gun that left his hand during the crash. Before he can even get his bearings together, someone from the charger wearing a green smiley-faced mask jumps on the driver's side of his truck, opens the door, and points a rifle at him. "Get the fuck out of the car," he yells with a weird foreign accent. "The boss wanna see you, ALIVE!" The man shouts after a short pause, then continues with a thick accent, "but act out if you want, and I'll put a slug in your head, and make this bullet sang a tune.

Stacks looks up at the person holding the Russian AK in his face, then peers out the front windshield and realizes he won't be winning this battle with his bullets, but with his brains. So, he yells out "Hey man, fuck it, fuck it. Take me to your jefe. But tell me this, what does your boss want from me?" "I don't answer to you nigger, so shut your big monkey gorilla mouth before I cut a hole through your throat and pull your tongue through it." "If you smiley-faced motherfuckers wanted to kill me y'all would've done it by now. And I bet my life cost more than a disposable fuck boy like yourself. So, hurry this shit up, and get me to ya boss motherfucker. Oh, and if you don't mind, I need a hand getting out of this bitch. I'm sort of in a bad position."

The guy standing in the car laughs and says something to his counterparts, in what seems to be Russian. After the laughing stops from the group of four. One of the guys who had been standing in front of the car steps back lifts his gun, and shoots neatly placed bullet holes up the left and right side of the glass, causing the windshield to break, forcing Stacks to roll out onto the ground at his captor's feet.

Chapter 1
Young
Reese

One Saturday afternoon in Richmond, Virginia, an aspiring rapper called Young Reese smokes on some top-shelf pressure and rehearses while waiting for his uncle to pull up at his mother's house. This night was no normal night. Tonight is the night of his first big performance since blowing up on the Gram. Since making it Instagram famous, labels all over the nation have been knocking on his door.

The one who's making sure all the shit is in line has been Young Reese's uncle, Stacks. Stacks and his baby brother Apollo, Who is Young Reese's father, made a pact they would take care of each other's family if anything was to happen to one or another; unfortunately, Stacks' brother met his fate first.

Young Reese, standing 5'11", with coffee brown skin, dark brown eyes, and a scar over his right eye he received in his younger years of thuggin'. He still looked younger than he was. Just turning 21 and still had his boyish features. Because of his dedicated work out plan, he has an athletic body that makes females of all ages go wild. Reese does a once-over of his custom outfit, Stamped with his uncles' management imprint.

(SMOD) (STACK MONEY OR DIE)z

Right on cue, his uncle texts him.

[*"Yo youngin... pulling up in 10 min. Be ready, we gotta roll!!!" *]

With a smile, Reese responds.

[*"Say less unc, born ready! Shit, I'm just waiting on you!!!"*]

His phone's ring tone sings his newest single once more.

[*"That's what I like to hear, View you $oon"*]

Ten minutes away from his nephew, Stacks turns the setting back to audio on his touch screen dash in his G500 Benz truck.

As he makes eye contact with himself in the rearview mirror, he reflects on that dreadful night when that muzzle flashed, and his brother's life was put on the dashboard right in front of him. As the spark from the burner goes off in his head, he snaps out of a trance and regains focus on his driving.

"Fuck I'm almost here," Stacks says out loud. "Let me text this Lil nigga to come on!" But to no surprise, Young Reese is already outside waiting. Thinking out loud, Stacks can't help but think to himself, "Damn, he's even on time like his damn dad used to be." Thinking of his brother is a cruel reminder of how many people were crossed the night his brother lost his life.

Pulling up to the curb, Stacks Admires how much his nephew's style and choice of fashion could have been chosen by his dad if he was here. Young Reese hops in the whip but not before tapping his two feet together, not allowing any debris to be tracked in Stack's impeccably clean ride. Stacks reaches out to dap up his nephew. Reese returns the greeting, and the two, execute their signature handshake.

Soon as the door closes, Stacks pulls off in front of the house, circling out the coda sac. Stacks reaches over and lifts the mid-size charm that is resting on Young Reese's chest. Looking from the street, then to the chain, back to the street. Then back over and make eye contact with Reese and says to him. "Damn, my boy! Your dad's chain looks good on you neph" "yeah, I know unc, good look! I know if my pops was here, he'd be piped the fuck up." The two laughs.

"Naw, Reese If your dad was here, he will be proud as fuck." "You right-you right unc!"

Young Reese flips down the vanity mirror, to see how his father's chain compliments his outfit. He then unzips his vintage peanut butter MGM shoulder bag and pulls out a pouch of MONEY BAG RUNTZ and a pack of Russian Cream Backwoods. Then says to stacks, "I hope my Pops is looking over us tonight, and bring me luck so I don't forget my lyrics." Stacks laughs then throws Reese a copy of Forbes's top 100 Black influential figures magazine, then he rebuttals. "You not gonna need luck for dem lyrics, my boy, go ahead and roll that gas up on that magazine, while I load up ya playlist for tonight."

Stacks and Young Reese blast his tracks from the Bose system in the Benz the rest of the ride to the show. All the while, Young Reese was live on IG, as he rehearses his rhymes, in the luxury hot box.

Chapter 2
Lil Nie Nie

After a whole day of skipping school with her best friend, LA 'Niesha (a.k.a. Lil Nie Nie) and Angelica (a.k.a. Jelly) sit at the top of Churchill in Richmond, VA at Chimborazo Park. Both take hits from their vape pens, infused with THC, and smoke while enjoying the view of the city's skyline. They can't help but imagine themselves, hitting the city tonight in their new outfits that both girls worked so hard swiping today.

"Bitch, I can't wait to see your big booty ass in those Prada jeans! They look like something a white girl would wear," Jelly says to her bestie with a smile.

Lil Nie Nie shoots her a serious look and says "I wouldn't care if it made me look Chinese, especially the price they cost! And I ain't pay shit, all I had to do is swipe a piece. I'm going to make sure them hoes hate, and all the niggaz jaws drop. And **All For Free**."

(All For Free) is the two-girls motto, and they plan to live those words until the day they D.I.E.

Recently they have been skating around Richmond and shopping till they can't anymore, all off the money of their victims, suffering from credit card fraud. The other day, they almost came close to getting caught by Lil Nie Nies's mother. Detective Brown of Richmond City police department, who one day ran across something she had never seen before called the dark web on their home computer. The sites used in their case, are to purchase the pieces (stolen credit cards) that keep them ballin'.

Lil Nie Nie easily convinced her mom that a boy from the neighborhood found a hook-up on replica designer clothing from overseas, temporarily explaining the fine fabrics that the seasoned detective easily questioned regularly.

Lil Nie Nie snaps out of her daydream and looks at her friend. "Jelly, sis, we have to make sure we stay on point and out of the city where my mom works. We can't swipe no pieces in my mom's jurisdiction." Nodding her head, Jelly says "I know sis, but you say we have to stay out of the city, what are *we* gonna do tonight if we suppose to be hitting the Lil Boosie show tonight, downtown in the city." Lil Nie Nie scratches her head trying to think, then Jelly gets up and does a dance and grabs Lil Nie Nie by the hand, pulling her up off the bench then they start to twerk. "okay, okay, look jelly, I heard on power 92. The first fifty females get in free, and on top of that, you already know every nigga up in that bitch gonna wanna buy us the bar, so we don't get to swipe shit tonight" "yes, bitch preach" Jelly responds. Then without skipping a beat, the girls holler out in unison. "All for free!"

They puff away and get geeked for another hour or so, talking about who they may meet later that night while admiring the merch that they acquired on their latest stain.

Chapter 3
Choose 1

After stepping off the stage, Young Reese is followed by Joe-Joe and Rell, his two day 1's always in front and center of his quickly growing entourage. With security escorting them to the backstage parking lot, they see Stacks cooling calmy while waiting for them. Leaning on his whip parked outback of the venue, lined up with several tour buses and back-to-back luxury cars. "Your uncle is right over there." The huge security guard looking like a linebacker says to Young Reese, while motioning towards Stacks.

Reese daps him up and says "Cool my guy. I appreciate your presence and all, but Young Reese don't need no security. This is my city, and this right here is all the security Reese needs." Young Reese says in 3rd person as he flashes a smile, revealing his top and bottom 18k gold permanent grill, while in the same motion lifting his shirt showing his compact Glock 19, custom airbrushed with Stack Money or Die.

"My uncle gave me this after my dad got killed. My pops might have been lacking, but I ain't. And If all goes wrong and even your big ass can't save me, I got this." Young Reese laughs and pats his tool with his right hand while holding up his shirt with his left. "This will be my savior."

The security guard laughs and says, "you know what's better than one gun? 2 guns." He then pulls open his blazer top, showing 2 holstered smoke gray 50 cal. Desert Eagles. All three guys including Young Reese jokingly said "daaamnn." And pick up their pace, sprinting off playfully.

Stacks greets the hyped-up bunch as he steps away from his G-wagon. "Whats happening fellas, I see y'all met Clarence, And it looks like y'all kicked it off well" Stacks says referring to his hired security. "Get used to him because he will be around for a while." Stacks takes a puff from his cigar and blows 3 rings into the crisp air.

"I enjoyed the show nephew." "How you see it, Stacks, from the inside of your whip unc?" Rell answers before stacks can. "let me tell him Stacks! Dawg you had 10k plus views on IG when you went live. I can bet Stacks was one of them."

"Rell you damn right I was, but this the kicker fam, while I was watching several labels from all over were tuned in as well. One of them mother fuckas was Boosie, who you just opened up for. You ain't even know it, did you? Look Boosie said on live before he went on stage, he'd sign you on the spot! Then the nigga Boosie tweeted out just a minute ago, that he has a check for Young Reese for $700,000 right now if you sign... here look."

Stacks reaches through his window and grabs his phone, just as fast as he could, he unlocks his device with his face, he already had Boosie's twitter page up, showing them the post. "Oh, shit, this nigga for real," Reese says as he reacts with excitement! "Nephew, when you ever see me joke about some paper?" "Never unc, you right" "Damn right, I am, But now look...

Yo Rell, Livestream this shit and notify all Young Reese's followers, we finna go live."

15 mins later, the guys stand around and sip D'usse and puff on some pressure till the live views hit 5,000. Then Stacks brings his attention towards him. Stacks towering over the crew standing around 6'9" with a sharp hairline and goatee flexing like an older Keith Sweat and swagger on a trillion. He stares into the camera

of the iPhone and says to the world, "aye yo Boosie much love, thanks for sending out that tweet for my nephew. Young Reese is a smart man, just like his daddy was, and I know he will make the right decision, that's why I'm extending the olive branch and using all my resources to turn my management company into an incorporated label. Just like all rap labels, the CEO offers the potential artist something."

Stacks walks to the back of the vehicle and hits the latch on the trunk, removing a vintage peanut butter MCM bookbag. Once he had the bag, Stacks places it on the hood of the Benz.

"Nephew, this may not be a check with a lot of zeros, I have to offer you at the moment, but this is a token that ties us together as business partners and a lot of M's along the way!" Stacks reaches into the book bag and pulls out an $85,000 iced out, Stack Paper Til' I Die necklace and pendant. "If you take this chain, I vow to you nephew that I will help you reach beyond the stars. So like I said Lil Boosie, Young Reese is a smart man. And I'm gonna stand with him on any decision he make. So, nephew, I plan to honor any words that came out my mouth."

Young Reese weighs his options, with a mental scale going off in his head, as the IG views hit 70k, 80k, 90k damn 100 thou, Young Rease has officially gone viral.

Chapter 4
After Party

After getting turnt up at the Lil Boosie show, lil' Nie Nie and her partner in crime race to the after-party being held at Club Mansion. As the girls break curfew, each girl texts their parents to let them know that they would be staying together for the night. Unlike Jelly, lil' Nie Nie is a virgin, but she knows how to work her finesse to get whatever she needs from her opposing gender.

After hopping out their ride share, the girls strut up to the VIP line. Lil' Nie Nie, sits 5'4", with an ass like it should be on Love & Hip-Hop, and a face that resembles Keisha Cole on an essence cover. She nudges her best friend at all the men and women as they break their necks to see them.

"Girl if any of those niggaz is looking at us and want a piece of this, they better think twice because they can't afford us if they are standing in that long ass line," Jelly says as both girls laugh as they approach the bouncer.

The big security guard looks at the two frequent flyers and shakes his head. "Rick stop acting like you don't know us," Lil' Nie Nie says while reaching into her Chloe clutch bag. "I know big guy," Jelly follows up, while jokingly licking her lips and winking her eye.

"Girl you better stop before you have my ass in jail," Rick responds, knowing the two are under age but quick to club-hop with official fake identification. (purchased from the dark web). "Hmmm... let me see what you have here," Rick glances at both I.D's... "O.K., 21? Good... Hold up, Tasha... Nicole! What happened to Porsha and Pam from last week?"

The girls laugh out loud while looking back and forth to each other, then back to rick. "Y'all hurry up and get in there before someone sees you and tell your momma, and I be damn if she gone have my ass for supper!" Both girls politely snatch their ID, then thank Rick and glide through the entrance. They approach the counter to pay and check in their coats, Lil Nie Nie pulls out her piece (Cloned Credit Card) that has been hitting all day, swipes $1500 on the card, and head to their table as they watch the sparklers on the bottles move toward their section.

Hour later:

"Bitch, I can't stand another drink," Jelly says. "Bitch, who you telling, but if these niggaz keep spending, we gonna keep drinking," Lil' Nie Nie replies. "You right bout that child." They high five and both girls say, **All for free**, not missing a beat.

"Girl, Let's go dance," Lil' Nie Nie pulls her friend towards the dance floor. Picking a spot right in the center of the dance floor. The girls go so stupid on the dance floor for the next 3 songs, turning to the life of the party. As the 2 girls dance face to face while twerking on two dudes at the same rhythm. Lil' Nie Nie can't help but notice a pair of eyes burning a hole through her.

"Girl look over there at that fine ass nigga staring at us," Lil' Nie Nie whispers in her friend's ear. "Nie Nie, he's not staring at us, he's staring at you," Jelly replies. "Oh, my Gawd girl look at his necklace, that bitch on drip!" Lil' Nie Nie says to Jelly while busting it, with a whole lot of extra spice, knowing that her unknown admirer was watching.

"Girl wave at him," Jelly says in her friend's ear. "Uhuh, hell no," Lil' Nie Nie says bashfully. In one swift movement, Jelly grabs her friend's hand and waves it at the man entering the VIP with his guys. The guy waves back with a gold grill smile. "Ohh shit girl that's the nigga..."

Before Lil' Nie Nie could finish her sentence, the guy she was dancing with grabs her by the shoulder and spins her around. "Bitch you just gon' go and flirt with some whack ass rap nigga, while yall dancing with me and my nigga."

Before Jelly could grasp what was happening, the dude goes off and pushes Lil' Nie Nie into Jelly, knocking both girls onto the floor. Before the angry guy could lift his foot to start stumping her, Lil' Nie Nie pulls a straight-edge barber razor her father left her for times like this, before he started his bid.

Out of the corner of her eyes, she could see several people jumping the VIP partition, not knowing the outcome. Lil' Nie Nie slides the blade above the angry dude's right ankle, severing the man's Achilles tendon, and dropping him to the floor. Jelly hops to her feet and struggles to get both of them up. To Lil' Nie Nie's surprise, the ones rushing her way were the ones coming to her defense.

As the angry dude friend looks at his partner on the floor holding his leg, he yells "don't worry my nigga, I'mma get that bitch"... but before he could clutch his hammer under his shirt, Clarence, the security guard who was with the rapper ran up and was already connecting his fist with dudes button on his chin, knocking him out cold.

And just like that in a blink of an eye, 2 salty angry guys lay on the floor as the damsels in distress got swept away by the up-and-coming rapper before anything else could pop off.

Chapter 5
Waffel House

Young Reese and Lil' Nie Nie sit in the back seat of Stacks' whip, talking about what just happened as Stacks drove the truck through the city using precise engineering. "Yo text your girl, she better keep up with the kid," Stacks says over his shoulder referring to Jelly. Jelly is following them in her car with Joe Joe and Rell.

"Aye unc, let's go to Waffle House, your nigga ribs bout touching." "You right nephew, it's about that time, ya heard me," Stacks says as he continues his maneuvering down Broad St. clutching the hammer.

"So who taught you how to handle yourself like you did back there," Young Reese asks Lil Nie Nie. "I don't like to talk about him, I mean my dad and all, but I do owe you a little kick it, for what y'all did back there," Lil Nie Nie says.

"It's nothing Lil mama, that's just what we do... protect what's ours, and from what I saw, I'm damn sure i want you to be mine." "I hear you boy," Lil' Nie Nie says with a smile and carries on.

"But on some real shit, my dad was my world and he taught me everything I needed to know when it comes to defending myself. He had to because he knew that he wouldn't be here to keep me safe in this war zone, we call the streets. But now he's doing a 20-year bid on a murder charge, I think a drug deal went bad. My parent sort of kept things about his case away from me. My mom was so embarrassed because it almost ruined her career. On top of that, a scandal was uncovered during that investigation bout my dad. I still talk to my dad and see him, but those two hate each other for what they put each other through. Damn, I'm talking too much."

Lil' Nie Nie says while starting to realize she was tipsy and spilling all her personal life. "Damn shorty, you don't have to feel like that when talking about shit in yo life with me, you'll see that you can talk to me about anything. You can call me a good nigga and a good listener." "aww, that's so nice, let me find out you got all the right lines for the ladies! But for real, I don't like to speak on shit bout my family because it seems to fuck up niggaz heads from time to time." Lil Nie Nie says. "You fucking right about that." Stacks says as he eases into the convo letting them know he had been ear-hustling.

"Yo Reese you heard that neph, you got me out here, chauffeuring around, the daughter of some 12. Shawty better not get us tow off." "Y'all don't have to worry about nothing, Stacks I swear..."I hear you ma" Stacks says cutting his eye at her through the rear view mirror. "I'm a big girl and one thing is for certain, I keep my momma outta my business." " Yeah let's make sure of that." Stacks says while turning the music back up, to thump through the streets of Richmond. As they climb to their destination, Stacks cant help but think about who the hell her parents are

Chapter 6
Stacks

*I*f it wasn't for that night ten years ago when Stacks put all his chips on the table, he may not have been walking into one of his penthouse lofts. Sometimes they are occupied with one of his soldiers trying to lay low with one of his women.

He couldn't wait for last night to be over he thinks to himself, As he opens the door and was greeted by his two blue English bulldogs, Stacks bends down and picks them both up after throwing his keys into the dish on the table next to the door. "Hey, Prince and Bella, what my babies been doin'?"

He pets them both on their heads then sets them down realizing it's 5 am. Stacks strolls into the bedroom to see his wifey sound asleep. He walks over to Talaya, pulls the comforter up to her chin, and kisses her forehead. With a groggy voice, Talaya opens her eyes and says. "Baby, how was the show last night?" "It was good sweetie, thanks for asking, but go back to sleep. I didn't mean to wake you up."

"You good baby, I missed you, so go get in the shower and come sleep next to me... One more thing baby. Did Young Reese take the chain?" Stacks put on a devilish smirk, bends down, and plants a kiss on her forehead, then turns around and exits the room, he pauses with a smile showing off his icy white veneers and says to Talaya "I didn't me in here with blood on my clothes did I?"

Before he knows it, he is in the shower letting steam roll off his body, Stacks takes that time to reflect. He glances out his two-way mirrored glass window overlooking the south of the James.

Back in the day, Stacks and his brother Apollo used to pull their whips up to the James River, and talk about how they would one day lock the city down. The only thing was that they both had different plans in play. Once they got the dope game on smash in the city Apollo would have the North and Stacks would have the South. Apollo had the plug and wouldn't budge on revealing the connection. The two brothers would be known to feud over the prices. When fentanyl came into the picture, the prices got cheaper and the dope got stronger, but Stack's prices stayed the same. Shit just wasn't sitting right with Stacks.

As the technology evolved and transactions would be made through cryptocurrency. That made Apollos plug even more untraceable. Both brothers' pockets were stuffed, but it wouldn't take a rocket scientist to see Apollo had a million dollars in Bitcoin accounts; steadily growing. Stacks snaps out of his daze just before he started to dwell on the events after that, which changed his life.

Stacks cuts off the water, dries off, and walks back to the room to let off some steam in between his girl's warm thighs.

Chapter 7
Moms Crib

*I*t's 7 am and Lil' Nie Nie is just getting in the house. When she walks through the threshold, she could smell eggs and bacon cooking, and hear Steve Harvey's Morning Show playing on the radio. Lil' Nie Nie kicks off her shoes and allows her nose to lead her to the kitchen.

"Woo child, I almost shot your narrow ass, don't scare me like that, make some noise when you come up in here" Paula yells over the radio. "Alexa, turn down the volume....

"Why the hell are you home so early La'niesha and why are you still dressed up looking like last night?" Her mom asked. "Ma ma mama," Lil' Nie Nie stumbles over her words trying to catch herself. "Laniesha, save it, child. I swear the longer your dad is gone, it's like you don't even care no more. The way things are going I know you not going to make it to college." Her mom said to her. "Mom please."

"No I'm tired of your shit and if I get one more Email from your teacher talking about you missed school again, I'ma send every damn police officer in the department out to find ya' black ass. Keep playing child, and your ass going to be right in there with your dad. Mark my words" She said angrily.

"Yeah, you would like that, wont you?" Lil' Nie Nie said while turning around to hurry away from her mother. "Bitch, I know you didn't just come out your body with that shit, you know what, that's why your ass ain't gettin' nothing to eat. You better fix it yourself." Ms. Paula yells to her daughter. "Fast ass little Heffer." she utters to herself. "One day I will catch your ass red-handed. Keep thinking you slick" Paula concluded.

After bathing and catching some sleep, Lil' Nie Nie wakes up to hear her mom leaving the house for work. She springs into action, running into the computer room half-dressed. She moves the mouse around bringing the computer alive. A few clicks later... she is inside an encrypted file that holds the wallet with the digital coins her daddy left her in charge of. Looking at the crypto wallet on the screen always makes her heart drop, because it's always up and down like the stock market. And today it's up.

Thinking about digital currency makes her think of her dad and the road he had to travel to get the crypto sitting in front of her. She wonders if it was all worth it even though it landed him in the pen, and his family fatherless. Lil' Nie Nie ended up learning everything she needed to about the dark web and cryptocurrency from her dad through letters and jail visits. His knowledge taught her how to scam so his cryptocurrency wouldn't be exhausted by the time he was released.

Her dad's name was Smoke. He built his empire off selling dope and laundering his money with Bitcoin, All while owning and operating barber shops and laundromats throughout Virginia . Smoke made the biggest deals he ever made through Bitcoin.

Then one day on a bad deal, he was shot twice and woke up in the hospital with a murder charge. Once out of MCV Hospital, he was sent to the city jail. Then he realized that his play had sent the money in advance. During the transaction they both got double-crossed before he could send the money to his plug, the person that tried to kill him, also set him up for killing his buyer.

Smoke lost twenty-five bricks of heroin and twenty-five bricks of fentanyl, but kept the money for the lost load, not forwarding his plug shit. Since then, the money increased in the Bitcoin wallet until his Lil' Nie Nie, as he calls her, was old enough to access the account. So, he fed her the game from then on...

Lil' Nie Nie smiles as she sees that the crypto price is up $3,000 today, putting her wallet up to USD 3.5 million. She knows her dad will be happy when he checks his email on the Federal Inmate computer and how his Lil' Nie Nie has been doing lately.

As she continues to stroke the keys on the keyboard, she receives a text:

[Young Reese]: Can't wait to see you again

[Nie Nie]: Emoji ♥ ♥ ♥

[Young Reese]: Meet me at the spot, recording studio – tonight at 11 pm

[Nie Nie]: OK will do, be Safe!!!

[Young Reese]: You too

Chapter 8
R.1.C.H.C.1.T.Y/Studio

[Hook] [2x] I hustle to get rich / You hustle to get by R.I.C.H.C.I.T.Y.

Catching plays all day / Hitting licks all night R.I.C.H.C.I.T.Y

[Verse]

I'mma hood nigga / street nigga / Gilpin Court representa

Try me If you wanna / to yo life it will be detrimental

Outcha front and center / Just remember this

I ain't a hustler for nothing / I'm out here getting' rich

In the streets Young Reese respected

tho if they call the medics

From a bullet / A nigga catching

My fellas gone make shit hectic

I think I'm bulletproof

Never felt what a bullet do

I feel invincible,"

Cuz I Play by street principles

Washington, Lincoln, Jackson, Grants, and Ben
Franklin

Stacking paper til' I die / off rap money and
dope slangin'

Washington, Lincoln, Jackson Grants, and Ben
Franklin

stacking paper til' I die / off rap money and dope
slangin'

[Hook]

I hustle to get rich / You hustle to get by

R.I.C.H.C.I.T.Y

Catching plays all day / Hitting licks all night
R.I.C.H.C.I.T.Y.

Stacks and Joe Joe stand behind the engineer in the studio vibing, as Reese's rhythmatic flows glide across the beat. Rell holds the Nikon 600 on a stabilizer with professional movements. As Reese finishes up on the last take, he saw Clarence come through the door of the studio with his pretty young thing behind him. Reese motions one minute with his finger to her through the glass and Nie Nie nods O.K. with a smile.

Stacks can't help but notice Lil' Nie Nie's Givenchy jogging suit, and matching sneakers along with the shoulder bag. "How you doin' Lil' lady," Stacks greets Lil' Nie Nie with a polite handshake. "Hello Stacks, and hello guys." "Heeey," the guys say while peeping at how good Reese's new snatch looks. "Damn shorty you look even better than last night... Now I know why my nephew was acting like he was gonna go crazy if he didn't get to see you tonight!" "Thanks, Stacks... I can have that effect on people at times!" Nie Nie said with a wink.

"Yes you do miss Nie Nie," Young Reese said walking out of the booth... "Oh, I do huh?" "Yup! You sure do, can I get a hug? Young Reese goes in for a hug and says, Yo, where ya girl from last night, you know she could have come with you?" "She would have, but she had some business to take care of for us. She will come out next time." Lil Nie Nie says as she hugs Young Reese.

"OK bet, my niggas can keep any of your friends company when you come through, ya feel me?" "Okay Mr. Young Reese, but you won't see me with no other people... just Jelly."

"I feel you, got to keep the circle small. Fucking with too many fake ones, that's what got my dad killed."

Stacks cuts into the conversation changing the topic. "Damn right, that's why a wise man told me you gotta keep the grass cut! Ain't that right neph?" "Hell yea Stacks, snakes don't mind snaking a snake." "Damn right and we all got a Lil bit of snake in us somewhere, so we snake them before they try us, and be careful if they try to join us." Everybody laughs as Stacks and Rease dap up. "But on another note, tonight I told Young Reese to invite you out with us, so y'all can better get to know each other! So Lil' Nie Nie, have you ever been to a strip club," "No, I can't say that I have." "Are you old enough young lady?" Stacks runs his eyes over the young tender Nie Nie and thinks to himself, she can't be no more than 17.

"Stacks, my ass was old enough to be up in the club with y'all the other night won't I?" Lil Nie Nie says as she poses with her hand on her hip. "Okay, okay don't shoot me shawty, I was just looking out for my tinder dick Nephew!" "Go ahead with that shit Unc!" Young Reese says as he plays and shoves his uncle. "But naw, for real Lil Nie Nie, I got a performance to do tonight at the Candy Bar.

After my show, I figured we can chill in that bitch, and throw some bread on a few working girls together, my promo team gonna be putting that work in and the DJ suppose to spin my shit all night." "Sounds like a bet, better not no hoes get out of pocket in that bitch." "You've got nothing to worry about, that big motherfucker from the other night, Clearance, my security? He's gonna be right there with us incase anything pops off!" "Okay Young Reese I can work with that"

"Call me Reese, leave the young for the Groupies." Lil Nie Nie smiles and nods her head, while the two get lost in each other's soft stare.

The group of people talks for another hour or two while the engineer mixes the song they just recorded. Young Reese escorts Lil' Nie Nie to the bathroom, and Stacks uses those several precious minutes to find out who the young lady is. Stacks goes into her pocketbook. "What do we have here." Stack's eyes get big as he thumbs through several fake I.Ds and a dozen of embossed credit cards, ready to be swiped at any given minute.

Chapter 9
Apollo

Apollo 12 Years Ago

After dozens of meetings, Apollo connect is still inquiring about who it is helping him dump the bricks so fast. As Apollo sits at the Rocket landing on the James River. Apollo was trying to figure out how to work this new digital currency called bitcoin. He just wired $100,000 from a bank account and is now waiting for notification that the funds landed in the digital wallet. Apollo's phone is just a reminder of how much he is being pulled from every direction, as the phone won't stop ringing. On top of that, his plug is on his ass about sending money through this untraceable coin. His brother Stacks is down his throat every time they talk about prices and products, not to mention all the people with their hands out.

Apollo is always on high alert, and he knows being paranoid comes with the street life. He goes by the saying "rather caught with it than without it." He slides his pistol from under the laptop sitting in the passenger seat, just as a bum taps on the driver's window. Apollo clutches his Glock 19, then hits the automatic button for the window to come down.

"You picked the wrong one to fuck with nigga, I got no change so you should get the fuck up out of here!" Apollo screams with the hammer cocked and points at the man's upper body. "Damn youngin don't shoot the messenger." The panhandler says with his hands up like it was a stick-up. "The hell you talking bout, ol' head? Talk before I blow this bitch!" Apollo said again.

"Look right over there," the panhandler pointed 5 cars down to a dark Blue Crown Vic with all blacked-out tinted windows. It looked like an undercover police vehicle. "What is this, some sort of setup? Man, I'm out of here." Apollo puts the gun in his left hand and reaches to throw the car into drive. "No no, wait" the man pleads. "That cop over there paid me good money to bring you this." The man passes him an envelope he had stuck in the front of his worn-out jeans. Apollo takes the envelope and rolls the window up and motions with the hammer for the guy to get lost.

Apollo looks as the police cruiser eases out of the parking lot and the crackhead dips off and slowly fades out of his view. Apollo rips open the envelope and pulls out a piece of paper, and it reads:

> 'What up friend, this is Smoke. I'm looking forward to meeting your business partner. Just like you are probably wondering who's this police officer bringing me messages... I wonder who is helping you move this product. The man who delivered this letter is my business

partner and you will meet him sooner than later.

P.S. send money to this Bitcoin address and I will see you once you have your affairs in order. Address: 8B3114Y95699105ZA3

Soon as this letter comes to an end Apollo looks at the crypto wallet on his phone. (006.15BTC). His heart hits his stomach because the money finally hits the account. Apollo ponders out loud, "Damn, Smoke even has police on his team and keeping track of where I'm at. What the fuck else does he know about me?" I got to get a few steps ahead of this motherfucker! Apollo sits and brainstorms a little more while he forwards the re-up money to his plug-through Bitcoin.

Chapter 10
Scamming
Pays The Bills

"*D*amn Girl I had a ball with you last night," Young Reese comments to Lil' Nie Nie referring to the good time they had at the strip club the previous night. "I ain't think you could keep up with me and the fellas the way you did shawty, and for real for real, I'm impressed."

"Boy, please that lil' money won't nothing, besides I have seen enough of them big booty hoes in music videos to know how they act around y'all rap guys anyway." "That money won't nothing huh? Well, Lil' Nie Nie tell me this, what do you do for money? because you spend it like you are a trust fund baby or something." They both laughed, as they passed a stuffed backwood back and forth. "No Reese, I'm still in school if you must know." "What the hell, I should have figured that ma, high school or college?" "College boy, I'm studying business management and financial literacy."

"Ooh Okay, but what do you do for money? Ain't no way financial aid got you stunting this hard." "I got a few hustles if you must know."

"Like what?" Young Reese asks while poking her in the stomach." "Reese, stop playing, what I look like giving up what I do." "You look like my boo who knows she can trust me with even her darkest secrets. Ain't like I'm gonna run and tell your supercop mom, or do mommy take care of you?" "No nigga, she wishes she could eat like this, as much as she is all up in my shit, busting my balls one minute then turn around, and then be trying to rock my clothes and shit. All I do is laugh" "Does she know how you make your money? Or are you just one big mystery to everybody." "Boy, you're not about to give up, are you?"

"Nope, that's one thing I can't do, I don't take no for an answer." Young Reese palms the back of Lil' Nie Nie's neck and brings their face towards one another, leaving their lips within less than an inch apart. "I I I..." Lil' Nie Nie stutters under her breath, as her eyes lock with Young Reese's, "I what baby, tell me!" "I I I, scam!" Nie Nie says bringing her tone up a few decibels. And Young Reese's eyes light up like a star on top of a Christmas tree.

"Now I know why I fuck with your ass so tuff shawty." The two locked lips and turned it up a bit. "Everything about you turns me on Nie Nie," Reese says finding a few words between a breath of air during their passionate moment. "You too Reese, but if you don't stop you gonna get me in trouble." "From the sound of it ma, me and you gonna have trouble as our last names!" The two continue to kick back and build passionately talking about life and cooking up ideas to get rich. There will be no limits if they can combine both their lanes of income.

Chapter 11
Sneaky Lil' Bitch

1 t's been 2 months since the argument between Paula and her daughter, but the word in her unit is that a file about Lil' Nie Nie is being passed around regarding credit card fraud and identity theft. The word is that she is linked to a local organization, that's been seen in the city living it up, and above their means. As one of the detectives from the cybercrime unit said. "Not your average local jokers."

To get to the bottom of things, she had no choice but to hire an old friend and retired police detective, who started a P.I. and security firm. This man is no stranger to Paula, they became well-acquainted when he helped undercover the web of illegal shit her husband was tangled in. And separated Paula from it before it got her kicked off the force.

Walking into the building at Paragon Place, Paula steps off the elevator and heads to suite 3b on the west wing. The door reads Big Clarence –

Security LLC. Paula walks in and is greeted by a PYT secretary. "Hello, Detective Brown. I will let Big Clarence know you are here." "Thank you, Laura. I love your nails"

"Thank you, girl! Whoever did yours won't playing no games either. But for now, you can have a seat, if we get a few minutes, we can exchange our nail techs info, because you and I both know, his tail is long-winded." The two ladies chop it up and 15 minutes later Paula was led to the office in the back. Clarence greets Paula with a hug and dismisses his receptionist.

"Paula, have a seat, what I'm ready to show you may be upsetting." Clarence turns down the lights and points his tablet projector at the wall. "So look Paula, these are pictures of your daughter and her girlfriend along with a group which has been tied to drug distribution and racketeering and now fraud. Also, all that shit is supposedly covered up by a music label."

Big Clarence thumbs through photo after photo, all taken by him and his staff that were on jobs working for Stack Paper Til' I Die record label. "Oh my God Clarence, I told that girl all the time to tighten up or she is going to end up where her dad is, I never in my life thought she would end up like this." Paula's eyes started to water as the magnitude of the situation start to build on her.

"Paula, don't fly off the deep end. We don't want this to end up like your husband's situation. And for the life of me, I'm not going to let that happen. Now I need you to wait til' I give you the go before you even bring this up to La'Niesha. I got a team working front and center doing security for this organization. And I want your daughter in the clear when this shit comes to a head." "Okay Clarence, I can't lose my baby to the system. She's all I have, and God knows I can't stand to have these allegations spread through my precinct like the last ones did." Paula sobs. "I'm gone help you do whatever it takes to get things back to normal for you."

Big Clarence raises the lights to a brighter setting with the controls on the tablet. Then brings Paula into his arms and says. "I've been taking care of you since Smoke got arrested and I'm not going to stop now." Paula buries her head into the burly man's upper torso. "I know you have Clarence, I know you have."

"Look, baby, one more thing I need, for us to crack this thing wide open." " Okay Clearance what is it?"

"For me to bypass any search warrants I normally would be able to obtain, I will need your permission to access your home video security, computers, and any digital devices Lil' Nie Nie may be using. So we can have a better look at where La'Niesha stands in all this, on the other hand, this might just lead us deeper than we ever could imagine." Paula grabs a tissue off the desk, dries her eyes, and then says, "OK Clarence, go ahead. Whatever you need baby." Big Clearance pulls Paula in for another hug and embraces her in his arms, at the same time glancing with a smirk at the privacy permission form on his desk, his PYT had drawn up before Detective Brown stop by.

Chapter 12
Run It Up

6 Months Later:

"**D**amn Lil' Nie Nie, this shit is sweet as fuck. I ain't know we could run it up this easy." "Boo this is just the beginning, wait until Jelly and Rell finish installing the skimmers around the city," Lil' Nie Nie said to Young Reese as he hits the button to push the sky roof back on his new S650 Benz. The two have been swiping pieces all up and down I-95. They decided to stop back in Georgetown's Diamond District in D.C. on the way back home.

"Boo, you trying to tell me that those little devices are all we need to get people's credit card info?" "Yes Reese, you have to trust me, I've been buying card info off the dark web for a while now. I'm almost sure, most of the vendors I purchase the information from are selling me skimmed dumps!" Young Reese scratches his head. "Skimmers dumps, and not to mention all these encrypted sites and accounts, this shit starting to make my head spin!" Reese said as both of them start to laugh. "Boo all you have to do is spend this money and stack the paper you make off your rap career. Let Jelly, Rell and I take care of all the hard stuff Reesey baby"

Young Reese grins at himself in the driver-side mirror, looking at his 5kt diamond stud earring hanging off his lobe like a frozen booger. He straightens out the mirror, then looks at his young Dane and lifts the icy pendant hanging off her diamond choker resting on her chest.

"(All For Free), huh boo." Young Reese reads the words on the custom piece, which only she and Jelly own.

"That's right baby, all for free. Now let's find a dispensary and go get some weed..." They both look at each other with a smirk and say "ALL FOR FREE." Looking at the GPS, the address for the pop-up shop dispensary landed them on Florida Ave, at the Stash House head shop. The two walk into the store set up like a bong and paraphernalia outlet. They look around for a few minutes until they see a door that reads: (POT HEAVEN AWAITS YOU). Lil' Nie Nie and Young Reese flash their IDs to the man wearing a security shirt, with a green smiley face on it, standing by the door. The man checks their IDs and then allows them access.

Once inside, they were led to the stairs. You couldn't tell them that it wasn't a stairway to weed heaven. Passing them on the way in was a white lady holding a gift bag with a green smiley face stamped on it. After 30 minutes of looking at the strain in every glass display, Young Reese and Lil' Nie Nie settle on an ounce of Super Diesel, An ounce of Lemon Haze and a handful of edibles including gummies, Fruity Pebbles and rice Krispy Treats, and a glazed donut all with THC contents. Lil' Nie Nie attempts to pay for the goods as Reese continues to check out some bud through a magnified cube.

"$275 donation, mamma," the cashier says while starting to bag up the purchase. Nie Nie reaches into her oversized Louis bag and pulls out a Capital One credit card that was lit like the weed they are ready to blow.

"I'm sorry ma'am, because of the laws we can only take cash donations." the lady says as she points to the sign on the wall. "Whoa, Whoa, you mean to tell me our money ain't good in here lady," Reese replies, joining in on the conversation. "Sorry sir, it's not like that at all, Federal Laws doesn't allow us to bank our money yet so there is no way to accept your card." Lil' Nie Nie gave Young Reese a look that he picked up on fast.

"Well Ms. ahh, Tiffany," Reese says, zooming in on the girl's name tag. "We had to park a few blocks away just to get to your shop and I left any cash I normally would carry with me inside the car. I wish I would have known before we came all this way and wasted our time." "No problem sir, we can hold your order for you if you would like to go to your vehicle and retrieve the money, or you can use the ATM right over there." Tiffany the cashier pointed to the 2 machines by the door. "Okay Ms. Tiffany, hold that and we will see what's good."

Reese takes Lil' Nie Nie towards the ATM and acts as though they are pulling money out. Reese whispers into her ear and then nods towards a fire escape at the back window. Seconds later... Lil' Nie Nie slams the door shut, blocking the exit, then puts the 2x4 sitting by the door into the cradles, used to reinforce security.

Lil' Nie Nie then yells "Go ahead boo, hurry up!" Reese turns from the ATM back to the lady at the counter holding his Glock. "I need everybody on the floor!" Young Reese says while waving his strap around at the other 3 people in the store and then back to the lady behind the counter. No sooner do they hear the security guard that checked their IDs pounding on the door.

"Go ahead baby... get as much as you can," Young Reese says, being careful not to say his girlfriend's name. Lil' Nie Nie cleans out every glass display and what was beneath it by stuffing the merch in her tote. While Nie Nie works, Reese was busy stuffing band after band in his skinny jeans. Running out of time, Reese stumbles across one last find, 5 hefty trash bags full of freshly processed cannabis. "Aight boo that's it! let's roll!" Young Reese screams out as he continues to point his pistol at the robbery victims, then the two make their way down the fire escape, then sprint through the alley and make their way to the car.

On the way back down i95 south, Reese's dick gets hard as he thinks about how thorough his Bonnie is and how she is making him one hood-rich nigga. "Young Reese can't no one say you some cap rapper, because you are living that shit now." "That's right boo, Bonnie & Clyde gonna keep striking the iron, even when that bitch fire hot. Now look Shawty, just keep your eyes on the road, while I start to count this shit up. HA HAAAA...

Chapter 13
Plug Talk

L ife felt good, but Stacks had a little trouble explaining to his nephew that too much was at stake, to be hitting licks, all while not sounding too contradicting, but on the other hand, he had no problem taking the lead in distributing all that greenery his nephew just dropped on him.

Stacks pulls his car to the I-95 underpass, off the Maury Street exit. Still to this day, he chooses this place to reflect and gather his thoughts. Back in the day, Stacks and his brother Apollo would meet up at this spot on the James River to smoke blunts, and put plans into motion, as they looked at the skyline, and practiced the laws of attraction, by talking about one day running the whole city.

Those who knew the two would without a doubt, know where to find them if they couldn't be found anywhere else. Stacks checks his ledgers and tally's up his inventory. After doing his figures, he now knows that he is down to his last few bricks of raw dope and completely out of Fentanyl. As predicted, Fentanyl is now outselling Heroin, making it an issue for his distro to keep up with the demand.

Stacks checks the time, he has a few more minutes until his connect pulls up and gives him the new Bitcoin Wallets Address to send his money and secure the order. Stacks double-checks his account and with the price of his cryptocurrency up a few hundred dollars, Stacks's bitcoin account sits right under a million. Talking out loud Stacks says a prayer to his brother, who he can almost feel right there with him watching over him.

"God, I ask you to continue to bless me with the right moves, and Apollo, this could have been us together big bro, you know I would have played my cards differently if they were dealt any other way. But we both danced with the devil and one of us got burned. Being that it is you that's not here, I know it's you who set the path a blaze, providing me the light to shine on these mother fuckers."

Before he could say Amen, no sooner does the devil himself pull up. The tall Vin Raine look-alike steps out of his new model Ford Taurus. Stacks pops the locks on his super sport Range Rover and his long-line dope source steps in. "Clarence knock yo' big ass feet off before you get in here." "Relax before these two bad boyz knock yo' head off". Clarence says while flashing his twin dezzys. Clarence sits halfway in the SUV and claps both of his feet together, then puts his feet in the car and closes the door.

"What are we doing meeting here anyway Stacks, even though it was years ago, it still feels like I'm returning to an active crime scene." "I know but it's the anniversary of the night he was killed, so I feel we needed to pull up and show some kind of homage." "I can go for that but let's make it quick so I can start getting your order together." "Speaking of the order, Look I will need 20 bricks of Fentanyl on the next load. I got the bread for my normal 10, but Ima need you to front the other 10, just give me a few days and I'll send cheese ASAP. The streets not going for stepped-on Fent even if Heroin is the base cut. My client's customers are chasing the bummest nods for the best prices, I want to leave these other niggas in the city at the lowest spot on the totem pole. "

"Stacks, I will see what I can do, but with the supply and demand there's gonna be a surge in prices." "Fuck that Clarence, when we made our deal and sacrificed the two people standing in between the two of us, and got them out the way. You vowed that you would stay consistent with the cheapest bricks and I vowed to stay loyal to you. We both have made each other enough money so that both of us could change our lives and the lives of the people around us. We also started businesses with endless sights. So, picture how much money I made your greedy ass, and you think I'm gone stand around and let you keep dicking me on the numbers. But if you going to go higher on my loads, I will have to find other avenues." Stacks said looking Clarence right in the eyes.

"I wouldn't put it past you kiddo, if you crossed your brother Apollo for the money, I know you would cross little old me baby!" Before Clarence could say another word, Stacks already had his Kimber 357 to the man's temple." "Don't ever put my brother's name in your mouth. You approached me with a plan to get us ahead. I've been telling myself for years that my brother was just a casualty of war, now you want to sit here and rub my nose in some shit we both stepped in, it's you who is not holding up to his end, you must got me twisted."

Clarence looks at the chrome handgun then back into Stacks eyes. "I thought you would have learned from Apollo, not to pull a gun if you, don't know how to use that bitch." "Fuck you nigga I warned you once, don't mention my brother's name, I'm not gonna warn you again. Matter of fact go ahead and give me the bitcoin address and you'll have your money in a short, just make sure you have your load on time." "Yeah alright mister big-time drug dealer slash mister record producer, aka so-called tough guy. I'm gone reach into my pocket...Please don't shoot" Clarence waves his hands in front of him pretending to be scared. He then reaches inside his blazer pocket and pulls out a piece of paper with the bitcoin address: 76ZB149Wf93110L40.

Stacks reaches for the piece of paper and Clarence snatches it back, "this is the last time you will ever pull a gun on me. Just remember I'm the one who secures you and ya little rapper buddies, and I know every move you and your little organization make and I can bring it all crashing down with the snap of a finger." Clarence gets out of the truck, balls up the address, throws it at Stacks and slams the door. "Bitch ass lil boy, don't forget I birth yo ass not your brother." Clarence says getting the last word. "Fuck you nigga, birth Dez nuts." Stacks says back not letting that happen.

Chapter 14
Ready To
Go Down

12 Years Ago

Sitting at his desk at one of his barbershops, Smoke just dropped his daughter La'Niesha, and her friend off at Virginia Center Commons Mall. He was using this time to handle his affairs with his supplier, who is on the way to see him. Smoke just received $100,000 from the only person he knows in the city that can move kilos as fast as him.

The money hit Smoke's bitcoin wallet, minutes after he got word Apollo had received the BTC numbers. Smoke used a police detective and drug associate, who went by the name Big Clarence on the job to keep an eye on Apollo. He wanted to make sure he wasn't going outside the fold to purchase his work, and to make sure he wasn't working with any of those alphabet boys. The main thing he needed to find out was the anonymous person Apollo is keeping secret, and distributing his drugs so fast.

Smoke glances at his security cameras just as his connects, undercover Crown Vic pulls up in front of his shop. Big Clarence strides into the establishment and headed straight to the back.

Clarence drops the duffle bag he was carrying, in the center of Smoke's desk. "Did that nigga send the money to the account?" Clarence asks, skeptical! He had been feeling uneasy about having their money transferred through this new thing called cryptocurrency.

"Yeah, the money is sent, I'm gonna give you the money for this load, so we can hurry up and prep for the next one. I just talked to Apollo. He gonna be ready for a bigger load fast, what he said was he is taxing 40 percent higher, whoever helping him move this shipment. And assured me he's gonna be ready in a few days for another one." "Sounds good Smoke, I've been making sure to keep my distance between myself and Apollo," Clarence said as he blows out 3 rings of smoke from his cigar. "I know! You have been doing a good job keeping a tail on him. But today that nigga was fucked up and wondering like a bitch who you was. He was like who was that mutha fucka in that unmarked car, that had a homeless man deliver the BTC address." Both men laughed out loud, then Clarence explains.

"Yeah, I had to find a way to get the message to him since you were busy with your daughter. I had to go and get Calvin, one of my washed-up informants. Calvin used to run packs for Chinese Rob back in the day, but when Rob took his fall, Calvin just fell to the wayside and picked up a bad crack habit. Along the way, I got the opportunity to flip him, I used to pay him well when he had decent leads, but as time went on...he could only put me on to small fish, so he barely got a dime from me. But today Calvin may have got off my shitlist".

"I'm listening", Smoke says, as he sits back in his office chair and rubs his palms together. "The snitch told me that he indeed remembered Apollo from back in the day on the block around Jackson Ward, and the word was that him and his brother grinded from an 8ball to a brick and never looked back.... the only difference between the two is one stayed on the streets and the other went to college. I guess that the person moving the bricks with him on such an organized level has to be his brother." "His brother huh, I wonder if the reason he is keeping his distro and his plug-in-the-blind from one another is that the numbers he pays will get exposed and they will link everything together."

"You know like they say Smoke whatever is done in the dark, will come to the light. Whatever the fuck it is Smoke, I'm going to surely find out." Clarence said as Smoke kicked back plotting their next move, not realizing it was already written.

Chapter 15
The Run Down

Reese slides through Nie Nies's house to check on things. "Damn boo, your mom got your crib set up like Fort Knox or something." "I know, she had all these cameras installed at our new house when my dad got arrested." "Damn bae, so is she watching us right now, she might pull up and spaz out! I ain't meet your momma yet, and I don't want it to look crazy, with her only child up in the house with some nigga she doesn't even know." Reese said with concern.

"Reese baby, let me do the worrying, and you just play it how I do. I swear when the time is right, y'all will meet. Come inside, boy! Me and Jelly is in there checking our skimmers. Her and Rell switched them out last night, at all the ATMs we put them on. It's really going to make your head spin when you see how many people ran their cards through our skimmers." Lil' Nie Nie led young Reese into the house where Jelly is already inside the computer downloading the dumps that the skimmers picked up when retrieved from targeted victims. "Hey Reese, what's up," "ain't shit Jelly, just trying to stay sucker free, in a world full of lollypop ass niggas." "I know that's right boy, I see you didn't hold back on your drip today," Jelly says, as she gives Reese a once over, taking in his designer swag and frozen neck and wrist. "You know, I got to look good to compliment my boo, this is just one of my fits for my video shoot we having later today. I told Nie Nie to bring you. I need some bad chicks in it to set that bitch off." "Thank you, Reese, and yes I will be there, but let's get down to business at hand real quick. Y'all come look.

Nie Nie and Reese huddled around Jelly at the computer screen. "Okay y'all, we have 340 accounts off the skimmers me and Rell put all around the city. Out of the 340, we have 213 credit and debit cards, with the Pins." "Got damn y'all some bad bitchies." Reese bearly utters a word because his jaw was damn near hitting the floor. "Yeah I know boy, I know Lil Nie Nie told you, me and your boy Rell already installed the replacement skimmers at the ATMs we got these from and some different ones. But look in that box right there! UPS Just dropped off the new skimmers we gone use on gas pumps, I been telling Lil Nie about. So when me and Rell link up tonight, we gonna go pick up the crack heads we be using to put them bad boys on.

Lil Nie Nie smiles and hugs Young Reese from behind and says, "Damn right boo, sis and Rell been working like a mothafucka, and I was thinking after you and Stacks figure out your schedule for the week, I can set up some meets, and sells some pieces to the folk who been burning my burner phone up for some lit cards." Everyone laugh and Jelly says. "No Pun bitch." The two girls high five and La'Niesha continue to talk to Reese.

"Boo, we can hit some ATMs and do withdrawals with the PINs. I know you want to hit some stores." "Damn Nie Nie, you and jelly got this shit down to a science. At the rate we going, we gonna need some people to work for us." "Boo, that's not a bad idea, because you know we got it hot with that job we pulled in DC," Young Reese chuckles.

"Pulling off jobs! Gurl, let me find out you want to make this a career." Jelly chimes in, "Y'all need to slow down and think a second. We don't need to be making it hot by hitting licks and shit especially when we got something that can make us rich right here in front of us...Besides Nie Nie, you already got millions in bitcoins saved up!" "Jelly what the fuck," "Oops, did I say too much." "Ahh duh, bitch gawd." "My bad sis."

Nie Nie shoots Jelly a wild look then explains to young Reese. "Look baby I'm sort of in a good position with money. All these scams I try to keep going, is just so I don't blow this money my dad left. I'm the only one he trusts to handle the account and make sure he is straight on his bid, and when he comes home." "Damn baby, I knew something brought us together. You are a rider for real."

"Yeah, boo you can say that, but I'm going to see my daddy in a few days. I wanted to ask you to go, but I didn't know how you would feel." "What do you mean, I'm cool with whatever, let me find out, am I supposed to be scared because he is in there for murder?" "It's not just that Reese, just the whole dad in prison thing is weird, but I figured meeting my dad first before my mom would be easier because I'm more like my daddy...besides being an alleged murderer and all."

"Who did your dad kill anyway?" "I thought you may ask that. It's nothing I'm proud of, but I just keep this news article saved as a rude reminder of where I came from." Nie Nie opens a file cabinet and pulls out a cut out from the Richmond Times-Dispatch. "Here read this". Nie Nie hands the paper to Reese...seconds later Young Reese finds himself stuck and frozen stiff as the article he's reading leaves his hand and hits the ground.

(RICHMOND TIMES DISPATCH)

Husband of RPD Detective, Stanley "Smoke" Brown, was sentenced today to life in federal prison for the murder of alleged king pin Apollo Rice.

Chapter 16
By any means

After eavesdropping on La'Niesha via Paula's home security cameras he was granted access to. Clarence ponders about what information will be uncovered if Young Reese was to make it to the visit at the penitentiary with Lil Nie Nie. Clarence knew shit would hit the fan if the pair ever found out about their coincidental ties to one another.

He now has to put the flame to the ass of his digital private investigator and personal hacker, white mike. He has to have him gain access to the files Lil Nie Nie has buried on detective Paula Brown's home computers. Clarence is hoping to find any passwords, or encryption codes for the sites BTC wallet where the money Smoke had left his daughter to manage after their last play.

Clarence now knows that his suspicion had been right after all these years. Nie Nie's best friend just helped confirm it. "So, Smokes baby girl had been holding on to the kitty all this time. Well, White Mike tell me you have something. You've been fucking off with that damn spyware, and thumbing through their hard drive half the god damn day. There must be a trace leading to that fucking bread somewhere. I need that mother fucking money." Clarence says slamming his fist onto the mahogany wood round table he sat at. He looked back and forth from the video feed he had projected on the wall, and to the computer screens white mike worked hard at. "Boss, calm down I am steps away from cracking these encrypted files, the girls are storing what looks like enough stolen credit card information, that if used right could bankrupt every banking and creditor institution in the United States."

"Listen, White mother fucking Mike, fuck all that, I'm paying you to find one thing and one thing only, and that's to find my motherfucking money. I don't give a fuck if you break every law that the supreme court ever passed. I need that god damn account. Hack into any computer, phone, or tablet that little bitch got. I don't give a fuck how long you sit at this desk, just fucking find it.

"You got it, Big Clarence, I'm not gonna let you down!" "I hope not because if this doesn't work, plan 2 is gonna have to go into motion. I just don't know how many enemies will surface." "I got you boss I swear." Clarence stood up and grabbed his 2-gun shoulder holster, holding his 2 50 caliber Blicks from off the back of the chair, and throws it on. He says "hit me as soon as possible White mike." "Gotcha Boss." He said as Clarence exits the room to prep his security team for tonight's video shoot.

Chapter 17
Video Shoot

1 t's 2:30 AM on Chamberlyn Blvd.... Outside of Good Times Bar and Lounge. Young Reese and the Stack Paper crew make this their last stop for the video shoot. Stacks had noticed Reese has been off his square all night. Stacks can't tell if Lil' Nie Nie has his head fucked up or if it is all the weed and lean that's got Reese so thrown. Stacks plans to pull Reese's coattail to everything soon as the time is right.

Stacks has been staying on point all night, after being alerted by Clarence to be aware of suspicious vehicles with DC tags, that keep circling the areas where they have been filming. The video director's assistant knocks on his truck's window to let Stacks know they need him in the next shots with Young Reese.

After letting the assistant know he will be ready in 10 mins, Stacks calls Rell over and hands him a shoulder bag with 5 switched-out

Glocks and tells him to pass them to all their folks, at the establishment. And to post a man every 30 to 40 feet, creating a perimeter around the video shoot.

"A yo Rell, do me this one fam!" "What is it Jefe." "Get Reese together for me bro, and tell him I said to get his Dick out the clouds or get it out that Lil bih Nie Nie mouth, If she is what has him off his rocker lately!" "Aight bet stacks" "And I cant stress this next thing enough Rell, I want everybody on point for the next scene. No No matter of fact, I need niggaz on their toes till we take it in." "Say no more, my friend, count me in, I'm on it!" "Alright Alright Rell, LOVE." Rell nods back with a smile and says "LOVE."

Stacks and Rell do the stack paper til I die handshake, then informs the director he will be ready in 5. The windows roll up on the Rolls Royce Cullinan, Stacks plans to gift the truck to Young Reese as a surprise in the video for all his good work. But if Young Reese don't stop slacking on the real business at hand, Stacks might repo that bitch soon after the video shoot.

Stacks can see out his peripheral view, left and right small crowds of people waiting to get a glimpse of what was ready to go down. In his rearview mirror, he can see 2 security guards, one to the front and another in the back of the Sprinter van Reese and Nie Nie are sitting in.

Stacks refocuses his sight in front of him. Clarence, his personal security, is on deck in front of the car. Looking at the devil himself, standing there to serve as his guardian angel, it is a rude reminder of just how far that man would go to protect what he thinks is really his.

****

Stacks can't help but reminisce about 11 years ago when he thought he was gone for good.... Stacks was on his way back from

Caroline County. His homeboy from the country had just scored 3.5 bricks of stepped-on dope for top dollar. This was his 3rd time that month making the trip. Headed home with $100k in his trunk under the spare tire, He made sure to hit the speed limit while hitting every turn signal.

When he hit the exit for Route 301, a blue Ford Taurus throws his lights on and hits him up. "What the fuck is going on, this got to be a joke." Stacks pulls the car over at a busy McDonald's towards the back parking lot. He races to take the clip out of his gun and throws it on the dashboard. He puts his hand on the steering wheel and cracks the window so the officer can speak through it.

Seconds later, the huge man with the green-lettered vest approached the vehicle. "Can you please step out of the car?" "What is the problem, sir." "I'll let you know soon as you step out of the car." "Fuck all that I know my rights." "Stacks can you please step out of the car, I don't want to ask again." "Hold up...what you just call me?" Stacks stopped before he could get another word out, and thinks to himself...whoever this cop is, he wasn't here to arrest him because they would have come with the calvary,

Stacks says. "Ok, I'm stepping out, just to let you know I have a weapon on board the car." "I know all about your registered guns, just relax and step back here to my car." The man who pulled him over was detective Clarence Jones with central Virginia's drug enforcement agency. And through his undercover work, Clarence realized Stacks was the key source to the distribution of the work that he supplied to Smoke, who had supplied Apollo. Unlocking a full circle.

Clarence let Stacks know he could directly supply any drug of his choice straight from the

D.E.A.'s evidence destroy department. The work had been seized straight from cartel syndicates, kingpins, and dope boys that stretched across all 50-plus states. And he had no issue getting it up the I-95 corridor straight to him.

Their conversation exposed the prices Stack's brother Apollo was getting per brick. Clarence painted the picture that the two of them could do better without Smoke and Apollo in the middle. Then Clarence leaves Stacks with a tuff pill to swallow, a plan to ex both men out of the mix.

Stacks snaps out his trance to the sound of Young Reese's voice as he opens the door to get in. "Unc, you good? You about ready for this last take." "You know what it is nephew! But do me a favor, put that blunt out I need you to focus..." Before Stacks could get the last word out, Clarence yelled. "Everybody down, GUN!

As he See's a vans sliding door open up with big ass guns hanging out them. "

A security guard grabbed Reese as he went to clutch his gun and sent him to the ground for cover...... FA FA FA FA FA FA FA tat tat tat tat.... And all you see is two men wearing green smiley face masks letting it ring out the sliding door of a blacked-out caravan.

As soon as the crowd started to frantically disperse away from the gun fire, another white man came from there right, wearing the same green mask, and caught the sea of people, from the side like a school of fish swimming right into his nets. He chopped his Russian AK right into the crowd. Gunshots sound for a whole 30 seconds to what felt like 30 minutes. Stacks open his door and slid out letting the engine block catch round after round. Stacks kept an eye on the opps movements by looking under the car,

As he walked down on him letting his assault rifle bark.

Suddenly the sound of the firing pin hitting nothing, indicated to Stacks and Clarence that their opponents were out of ammo, now its time to return fire. Clarence and his security detail rise from the dusk and let their guns fire.

As the man retreats to his getaway car, Clarence and his guys send 30 to 40 shots back in the same direction they were just coming from. Stacks jumps up from beside the bullet-riddled car and sends shots side by side, with Clarence getting a clear look at the tags, which appeared to be those same D.C. plates.

Stacks aims the green beam on the bottom of his gun, right between the shoulders of the masked man as he ran. A shot sent him spinning around, causing him to stumble right into the car. His boys pull him in and peel-off.

"Lucky mother fuckers, Reese you good Neph?," Stacks yells out, "Yeah I'm straight unc." "word im good too, what about u Big C? "Fellas what do we look like?" Clarence shouts to his crew to make sure all his men are accounted for. Each man sounds out one by one like a roll call, loud enough to be heard over all the yelling and screaming. Clarence knows with all the bullets that just got let off someone had to be hit. He races to the sprinter van to make sure the one person that held the lock and key to that bitcoin account was not hurt....

Chapter 18
Not Under My Roof

Channel 6 news

"*I*'m standing here outside of, "Good Times" on Chamberlyn Ave. and police reported that over a hundred rounds were fired last night, leaving one dead, and several people facing non-life-threatening injuries. Though we are waiting to hear more information about the incident. We do know the police are looking for at least three masked gunmen, who were last seen speeding off in a Late-Model Dodge Charger. The Richmond Police Dept. asks that if you have any information possibly leading to their arrest, please call the hotline @ 1-804-USnitch. Coming to you live from 1600 block Chamberlyn Ave. This is John Burnet...in Richmond. Back to you Candice."

Paula turns off the tv and stormed into the bathroom, just as Lil' Nie Nie was stepping out of the shower and about to grab her towel.

"Mom, what the fuck- I'm in here!" "You little bitch, I know you better watch your fuckin mouth in my house for real!" "Mom, what's the matter with you?" "What's the matter with me? I'll tell you what's the matter with me. First I get a call from Angelica's mom, asking if I knew y'all were with them trashy ass people that had yall in the middle of a shoot-out last night?

And second, she had to sign her daughter out of the hospital this morning, talking about Angelica was hit last night by bullet fragments." "Ma, ma, mama," Lil Nie Nie stuttered while trying to avoid eye contact. "Go ahead girl and get your lies straight. You really think I don't know about your little wanna-be rapper boyfriend, who got you out here breaking the fucking law child."

"Mom, OMG what are you talking about?" "You know what I'm talking about. This fraud thing you've been tied into for some time now.

Then come to find out you're bringing robbery into the picture. You gonna be looking at a hard time in prison, right there with your dad." "What, are you spying on me?" "As long as I live, I can do whatever I need to do to make sure I know what my child is doing!"

The things I found out about you doing out here La'Niesha has me questioning the oath I took. I swore to put people like you away for good, I don't know what to do." "Oh yeah Mom, is that right?" Lil Nie Nie said angrily as she stormed pass her mom, and went across the hall to her room.

"Hey mom, is that the same oath you used to put my dad away?" "Put your dad away? How dare you talk that bullshit to me La'Niesha!" "Bullshit mom, dad told me everything, he told me that if not for that little affair you and that jealous detective buddy of yours had. He damn sure wouldn't be behind bars right now as we speak, and now he was stuck in the Penn, feeling like his own wife had something to do with him being set up."

Paula's jaw drops, almost hitting the floor. "Why you ungrateful little bitch!" Paula raises her hand and swings towards Lil Nie Nie's face. With cat-like reflexes, Nie Nie puts her right hand up and grabs her mother's firey hot palm. "You know what little girl, because you got all the sense, in your grown ass head, let's just see how those ugly streets treat fast ass little girls who think they got everything figured out. I want you to get your shit and get out!"

"Get my stuff and get out? Okay, you only have to tell me once! Real quick though mommy dearest, I just want to give you a heads up before I get out of your precious little house. I don't think my daddy is gonna like how his sweet ex-wife decided to kick his only baby girl out to the curb. One more thing, I will make sure I tell him you said hello when I go see him tomorrow!"

"Is that supposed to be some kind of threat? Because if it is, tell him I said kiss my ass, since he wants to fill your head up with that bullshit. Oh, and uhh-Lil Nie Nie, as your dad like to call you, please don't call me when these oh-so-unforgiving streets eat you alive unless there's an I'm sorry and you told me so along with all the bullshit you about to get hit with."

"And one more thing," Paula said. "Aww, what now?" "Move faster, I have somewhere to be." Lil Nie Nie rolls her eyes as her mother exits her room and continues to get dressed, then storms into her closet and grabs an armful of her belongings and makes several trips filling up her trunk.

At the last second, she remembers one important thing. She rushes into the computer room and slides her thumb drive into the port. Nie Nie quickly downloads the software and encrypted folders that hold the passwords to her and her father's fortune.

Chapter 19
Visiting Day

*I*t was a long night for Lil Nie Nie, she rode around the city just smoking and reflecting on all the current events that have been transpiring in her life lately. She woke up in Jelly's drive way, face timed her and said she was outside her house. Once inside Lil Nie Nie had to check on her best friend and tell her sorry for getting injured. Then take a shower, and change before she and Reese took the ride for the visit to her dad. After making sure her rode dawg was straight, Lil Nie Nie began on her journey.

Soon as she pulled up to Reese's spot, she parked the car and jumped out to hug him. They embraced and held each other for a few minutes, then quickly remembered they had a 3-hour ride ahead of them. Before hitting the highway, Nie Nie stopped at Wawa and grabbed some snacks and backwoods while Reese filled up the car.

Their scenic ride flew past, they talked about what they wanted out of life and what the future look like for the two of them. "Honestly, baby fuck what Stacks got to say about us being together, for real- for real, and anybody else too. I have been studying the LAWS OF ATTRACTION. And I believe that shit brought you to me, and I feel like we should fight to keep what we have, ya feel me?" "I'm with you on that Reese but what if this visit flips what we have upside down?" "What do you mean Nie Nie?" "I mean what if my dad says something that you may not like." "Oh, shit boo I see but look though bae, I've already processed almost anything he might say, and I'm gonna keep my cool no matter what. I just want to hear his side of the story baby that's all."

"I know boo, I'm here for you no matter what, just know that Reese. But look though baby, we're almost there."Lil Nie Nie puts on her signal to exit for Beckley, WV. And it wasn't long before they are at the federal facility visiting her father. They went through the security procedures, then wait about 15-20 minutes. La'Niesha spots her dad as he parts his way through a sea of inmates as they enter the visiting area.

"Daddy!" Nie Nie yells as she gets up and runs and jumps into Smoke's arms. Smoke grabs his baby girl and brings her in close. "How's my Lil Nie Nie doing?" "I'm good daddy, you're looking good." "Thanks, baby you too, you're growing so fast, it's hard to keep up with you." Smoke puts down his daughter and steps back to size up the man that escorted his daughter to the visit.

Young Reese stares at Smoke and doesn't fold under the intense stare down. Smoke sticks out his hand exposing his muscular build and tattooed arm. Offering Reese his hand for a pound. "Daddy let me introduce you two, this is..." Before Nie Nie could get out the introduction Smoke interrupted and hit the nail on the head. "Apollo's son, Lil Reese," Nie Nie and Reese looked at each other. "What a small world, Apollo used to show me pictures of you all the time, he used to say he was grinding for your future. Man, you are a spitting image of him. May he rest in paradise. I know what you're probably thinking, but Apollo was my guy. Come sit down, I will tell you more. Reese shakes his hand then the three take their seats.

11 years ago

I had a trunk full of dope waiting for my number one mover to pull up. I started feeling a tad bit impatient, so I hit him up to see exactly where he was at. Seeing Apollo's Yukon Denali pull up made me feel at ease, I was already outside smoking a cigarette and preparing to forward the funds Apollo had sent for this shipment to my people, who were waiting for the bitcoins to arrive. I just needed us to complete the transaction and was about to do so. Apollo pulled up right in front of where I was standing, and hit his high beams, giving us some much-needed light at the underpass.

Me and your father dapped up then walked to the back of my car. I remember like it was yesterday what he said to me. "Yo, smoke I can't for the life of me understand why you got that police nigga on my ass tracking all my moves. I thought we were better than that, plus you stay down on me about meeting my people." I said to him "Apollo it's not like that, you got to trust me, I have no trouble introducing you at all, but you be so closed lip with who ya partner is, it's only right I do the same. But that shit got me low-key sketched out. But you do know how that shit is sort of weird to a nigga, right?" "You can call it what you want. I just call it protecting my best interest." "You're right Apollo, But if it means anything fam, you are a valuable player, with all this shit we got going on. See look; check this right champ, I'm willing to go the extra length tonight to make sure you are good. The guy you suspect tailing you is my supplier, so in all reality, he is your connect.

He's a DEA officer that keeps us loaded. That's why I want everyone introduced properly in the circle, so they can be protected under the umbrella that he provides for us. And by everyone, I mean you and your brother." "My brother! What do you know about my brother?" "I know that your brother helps you move them bricks as fast as you do, if you don't mind me saying." "I do mind you all up in my fucking business and that's some real shit Smoke. But if you must know, my brother Stacks would go into overdrive and not give a fuck who he serves, that's why I keep an eye on how he does business and who he do it with, so I tax him on the keys to slow his roll. The extra money I prop off him,

THE LIES WE LIVE WITH

I use to put him through college because the nigga is a different type of smart. So one day eventually me and him gonna be able to start businesses, and create generational wealth for our fam, like you Smoke."

"Okay, okay that's alright Apollo, maybe we can sit down, and all get on the same page." "That would be sweet Smoke, but my brother is just so big-headed and stubborn that at times, I feel that it would be best to just keep him on a short leash for now."

We talked for a few more minutes then the next thing I know, your father and I get ran down on by a man coming out of the woods holding an AR-15, that just heard everything we just discussed. Then that undercover police cruiser that was so familiar to us pulled up and Clarence big ass hops out. The man with the AR yelled at me and Apollo. "Put your hands up and don't think about moving."

There was only one thing, we couldn't move if we wanted because we were in shock looking at the two motherfuckers in front of us. Then Stacks yells out to Clarence "Clarence you was right, my own brother got a nerve to sit up here and tell this motherfucker he gonna keep me on a short leash, that motherfucker been rationing the supply. Just so he can tax me, for what? To pay for my school, just so I can get a degree and run a business that he wants to be able to say he owned. Bro, you got me fucked up."

"Stacks what the fuck." Your dad screamed out. "It's too late nigga, I saw enough and I definitely heard enough, so save it because me and Clarence gonna be running the show from now on." Then the man who I trusted raised his two guns our way, and I was like, "Clarence whatever you think you doing ain't gonna fly far, I still got your bitcoins and I know you won't kill me without getting that bread." "Well,

Smoke I came to get that work back from you since you want to drag your feet getting that money to me, and my new friend will take over your shipments." I was stuck lost for words then Stacks walks up and goes in the trunk and retrieves the duffle bags.

As Stacks was taking the work to Clarence's car, Apollo out of nowhere raises his gun-waving it back and forth from Clarence to Stacks. "Man, I should bang on both of you niggaz" Apollo says. "Stacks you better get your little bitch brother under wraps before I earth this motherfucker." Clarence says aiming his guns at Apollo. Next thing I know Apollo says fuck all y'all, backs toward his driver's side, and jumps in his truck.

In my head, I was thinking to do the same thing, so I draw my gun and follow suit that was when Apollo reversed the trunk then throws it into drive and aims the vehicle right at Clarence and Stacks. Those two then fires there weapons into the cab of Apollo's whip, at the very second, I up my pistol and let it ride, aiming it at the two men that just crossed us. Long story short I took two bullets in my pelvis area, passed out from loss of blood, and woke up handcuffed at VCU, with a murder charge for something I didn't do. I swear Lil Reese if I could've done anything differently, I would have. First and foremost, I would have never had Clarence look into who Apollo's associate was, things would have never backfired on me and Apollo. Over the years I learned that Stacks and Clarence lock down the city after Knocking me and your dad off our thrones."

"Well, Mr. Brown." "Smoke, call me Smoke." "Smoke I honestly believe your story, it's more of an explanation than what my so-called uncle ever gave me. And I know Clarence as well. Now I see exactly why he stays so far up my uncle's ass." "I apricate you saying that Reese, like they say its only room for one king, so keep an eye on Clarence, Because it's only but so long he can stand to share the top with Stacks."

Lil' Nie Nie and Reese chop it up with Smoke for a few more hours. As they head home with a hell of a pill to swallow, and so much on their minds, they are so distracted that they never pay attention to the car trailing them. Nie Nie tells Reese to pull over to the next rest area so they can use the bathroom.

Soon as Reese pulled the car into the parking space, a white sprinter van sped to a stop directly behind them. As the van boxes them in, Reese tries to grab his gun, but three masked men are already pulling him and Nie Nie out of the whip and forcing them into the back of the van. Where they are quickly duct-taped and bound.

Chapter 20
Lol Smiley Face

After sitting back-to-back blindfolded and duct-taped to their chairs for the last 24 hours. Young Reese and Nie Nie jump at the sound of the bay doors opening in the warehouse they were being kept. "Who the fuck is that and why you got us in here motherfucker?" Young Reese yells out to the unknown suspects. Then Nie Nie says "Yeah let us go, you bastard, just to let you know, if you do something to me, my mom will have every police officer in Virginia crawling up your ass faster than you can shake your dick after a piss, you faggot."

The two of them quietly fall silent after their angry outburst was drowned out by the kidnapper's laughter. "Fuck you, laugh all you want, let me loose and I will show anyone of you fucks the business." Lil Reese yells out mad as fuck. "Well, well, look who the fuck decided to grow some nuts, the motherfucker didn't act all tough the other night. The little motherfucker was on the ground covered up by security when them niggaz tried to take his head off."

"Clarence," both Lil Nie Nie and Reese said at the same time as they made out the voice. Next, the bright exposure of the fluorescent lights almost blinds the two as one of Clarence's henchmen rips the blindfolds off their eyes. "What the fuck you got going on Clarence, this is some fuck nigga shit you into man, let me and my shorty go." " HA HA HA let you and your little shorty go huh? That's real cute, and truth be told she is the real reason y'all tied up, in this dirty motherfucking building as we speak."

"What the fuck you want with her huh? Haven't you done enough, it should be the other way around, yo ass should be tied up, ready to meet your maker, for that foul shit you and my uncle did to me and Nie Nie's dad." Clarence nods at one of his men, and the man dressed in black walks over to Reese and punches him square in his face, leveling him over in his chair straight to the floor.

Clarence walks over to where young Reese lays and crouches down, then lifts Reese's chin with his gun. Bringing their eyes to meet. "Lil nigga if you knew anything, you'd know battles get won by the ones who stands the tallest. Wars come and go, and soldiers are disposable. So remember this, I haven't lost a war yet and I highly doubt your motherfucking ass is gonna stop me. So, get some sense and pick the right side."

"Pick a side? nigga I rather pick my grave if you think I'mma side with a nigga who killed my daddy. Fuck you." Reese jerks his head away, conjures up a wad of saliva, and hawks it right in Clarence's face. Clarence doesn't even flinch, he just brings down the pistol over young Reese's forehead like a judge and his gavel. "Night night you little bitch ass boy."

Lil Nie Nie can't help but yell out for him to stop at the top of her lungs, as she almost breaks her neck, trying to look over her shoulder at young Reese as he gasps for air with a light snore. "Stop! Why the fuck are you doing this? Tell me what you want from me. You already took my dad away from me, I'm not going to let you take someone else away from me." Clarence stood up and walked around to Nie Nie and whisper "Shh, quiet your pretty little mouth and let me do the talking,

I knew you were smart just like your mom, she wanted to help your dad before it was too late, he was already in deep shit. So Paula did what any smart person would've done in her case. And that was taking cover before her ass got burned. And it was nothing she could do to help her dear husband. And I can see just how much you want to help your boyfriend young Reese. So, I'll make this easy for you." Clarence reaches into the breast pocket on his jacket, revealing the thumb drive that white mike confirmed was the digital vault, he had seen her load before she left her mother's house. His guys ripped her car apart until they found it tucked away in her stash spot.

"I knew your dad Smoke had my money all this time. I just had to wait for the right time to get it back from him. Never would I have guessed he would have left it in the hands of his child. So, I guess it's gonna really be like taking candy from a baby." "Money, what money? And why are you holding my zip drive in your hand like its something important on it." "Ahh ahh ahh, I don't have time for games La'neisha, that night Smoke lost his freedom and almost lost his life, was the night I got tired of him toying with my paper for the last time. All he had to do was send me those bitcoins you have access to, and for Apollo to play fair with the loads.

Maybe your daddy wouldn't be behind the wall and his daddy wouldn't be dead." Clarence nods towards young Reese, and kicks him in his ribs just as he seems to have been ready to gain consciousness. "Clarence please don't hit him anymore, just tell me what the fuck you want from me." "That's a girl, I knew you'd be cooperative. So, let's get down to business then!"

Minutes later white mike came through the door with a mac book in his hands. Clarence walks over to where a pile of pallets was and grabs an egg crate and flings it towards their direction. It lands right in front of Lil Nie Nie. White mike sits the laptop down and powers up the system. Clarence inserts the thumb drive into the USB port and steps back and starts rubbing his mitts together.

"White Mike this is what it all boils down too huh, some computer files this little bitch had all this time. My gut was right all along, now hurry up so I can see what's inside this crypto wallet." "Okay boss I'm on it!" White Mike opens the folders that are located on the encrypted thumb drive, and an hour later he is still clicking here and clicking there. After a while, he was tired and just sat there with a stumped look on his face.

"Boss this bitcoin wallet is trapped behind a three-layered encrypted security wall, face recognition, voice verification, and that's linked to a phrase that needs to be said." "What are you saying? You assured me that you could hack into anything put in front of you." "Sir I can, I just need time." "Time is of the essence Mike, and I feel like you're wasting mine. From the sounds of what you just told me La'Neisha is the actual key to opening this wallet all along." "Yes, boss she is gonna have to fully cooperate to get this thing unlocked."

Clarence turns his attention to Nie Nie, "You hear what Mike said, I need your full cooperation to unlock your digital vault. So do I have it?" lil Nie Nie looks Clarence dead in the eyes and says. "Make his ass do what he is paid to do! When you had him spying on me to figure out where my daddy's money was, he should have had a better plan, because he knew this part of y'all little mission was coming." "A plan huh, I try not to plan much, because with plans sometimes come disappointment, sort of like now."

Clarence untucks his handgun and raises it to the back of white Mike's head, then cleans his top, sending a red oatmeal substance onto the laptop screen that set right in front of him. Nie Nie lets out a scream that was met with the echoes of the gunshot that had just rang off.

Young Reese awakes and starts to squirm once he realized he was laying in a pool of white Mike's blood. Clarence walks to young Reese and steps on his head keeping him from moving. "You see La'Neisha, I don't have time for games, now your little boyfriend is gonna end up another dead rapper if you don't cooperate." Clarence threatened.

Clarence nods to one of his men, signaling to him to cut the duct tape off Nie Nie that kept her bound. Clarence takes his foot off Reese's head then picks up the laptop and throws it on her lap. Immediately, he aims the gun next to Reese's head and lets off another shot. "I'm waiting La'Neisha, the next shot I guarantee not to miss."

"Okay stop, don't kill him, I'll give you the fucking money, but you better be far and gone when my dad finds out. Because when he does, he gonna eat you for breakfast, lunch, and dinner." "Bitch fuck you and your daddy, the only thing yo daddy gonna be eating is state trays around this bitch. Now hurry up and open that motherfucking digital wallet." "Whatever nigga. We gonna see about that shit mother fucker." "You right I did fuck your mother! So I guess I am a mother fucker!" "huh laugh now mother fucker, please believe you gonna cry later."

Nie Nie clicks around on the computer, then puts her face in front of the camera, allowing the software to read her face. Once that is accepted, she put her mouth closer to the microphone and says the phrase "All For Free" allowing the program to recognize her voice. The logo on the screen spins around and around as it loads. Seconds later, the screen brightness turns up as the software unlocks the account revealing 179.94679568 BTC worth a sum of $3,017,876.

Clarence's eyes widen as he stands in the center of the small huddle of people looking at the computer screen. "Jackpot," Clarence said as he reaches into his pocket pulling out his cell phone. Once he is on his device, he clicked on his photo gallery where he retrieves a screenshot of his bitcoin wallet's address. He zooms in on the digits and then throws the phone in Nie Nie's lap.

"Now La'Neisha, thank you for cooperating and getting us this far, there's one last step." "What motherfucker." "Right, once again, I did fuck your mother, but that's for a later discussion. But what you gonna do next is, send that cheese to the number in front of you." "Clarence, how do I know you're, not just gonna kill us after I do this? Once this goes through, please let me and Reese go, you cold-hearted bastard." She pleaded. "Bitch just do it, does it look like I'm in the business of making promises."

Young Reese, out of nowhere, rebuttals from the floor. "No nigga, more like in the business of crossing people, that's what you look like." Clarence reaches down and lifts young Reese by the neck while still taped to the chair. "You got 10 seconds or I'm gonna turn this nigga brains to some apple sauce." "Okay, okay stop." Nie Nie clicks on the feature that allows the account holder to send funds and then clicks on the first blank space that says enter amount. "How much," she asked. "Don't make me laugh, all of it." "My dad is going to kill you." "Fuck your daddy, now you got 5 seconds. 5,4..." "Hold up wait. I'm coming wait." Nie Nie punches Clarence's info into the sender page of the bitcoin wallet program. "Hurry up Nie Nie you still haven't sent it yet 3,2..." "Wait I just have to submit the voice verification one last time for safety measures and you'll have my fucking money." "You're wrong little girl." "About what?" She asked eagerly. "You meant to say MY MONEY."

Nie Nie sticks her middle finger up at him with a matching grit on her face, once the program asks for her voice she then parts her lips and says "All for" she takes a slight pause and Clarence stoops down a tad bit and whispers 3,2...before number 1 could leave his tongue, a Hummer truck slams through the garage doors followed by several men on dirt bikes all wearing green smiley face masks. Before Clarence and his men could react to what just happened, the men that just entered were all letting off their artillery at anyone who seemed to be in that establishment to harm Reese and Nie Nie.

Chapter 21
Continue of
Prologue

Speeding down Belt Blvd towards Broad Rock, Reese and Nie Nie sit in the third row of the truck. The three other occupants sit quietly on high alert, clutching the same guns that were just used to free them. Clarence had taken a bullet to his head, and if somehow survived, from the looks of it, now would be the least of their troubles.

Reese was the first to speak up breaking the silence. "Yo, who are you guys, and why the fuck did you just save us." The guys, who are still wearing the smiley face mask, just look at one another, from left and right but kept quiet. "Matter of fact, y'all them niggaz who tried to take us out the other night, I'll never get the picture of them fucking mask y'all got on, out my damn head shawty." The guy who sat in the front passenger's seat turns around and looks back at Reese and nods his head yes.

Nie Nie smiles at him and says, "Wow thank you for helping us, I don't know what may have given you a change of heart, and you decided to save us, but in my heart, I feel like we owe you ourselves." The same guy who responded to Reese spoke up and says with a heavy Russian accent. "I'm glad you said that miss Nie Nie because you do owe me."

He pauses for a few minutes as Lil Nie Nie and Young Reese look at one another puzzled then he says. "Do you remember me," as he pulls off his mask and stares at each other one by one. It only takes the two a few seconds to realize he was the security man who watched the door at the cannabis shop in D.C, the two had just robbed not too long ago.

The entire truck bursts out into laughter as they take in the surprised looks on those two faces. "Don't be so taken back now when you see some real Russian gangsters right in front of y'all asses. You two had a lot of balls when you decided on stealing my money and product, then jump out my window and making a break for it." The two sit there lost for words as the truck hits the highway on I-95 north.

"What, the cat got your tongues now? Well, I guess that's understandable, so I will do the talking. First off, my name is Francis Glockenspiel, and I own and operate 20 cannabis shops like the one you just so happened to rob. That day I was doing hands-on work at one of my busiest establishments. My associates and I realized that you two were worth more to us alive than dead, Especially considering the horseshoes that was up the asses of you and your better half, being neither one of you took a bullet when we came for your heads in that shoot out on route 301.

See after that night we tracked your uncle down, and he made me a reasonable offer I couldn't refuse. So, if it wasn't for him, you two motherfuckers would already be laying 6ft under, and let's just say, not right here next to me. So, this is how it's gonna work from here on out. Both of you two are gonna break down all your earnings 50/50 until I say I'm satisfied, on what you two owe me from that little escapade a few months ago.

Reese, you will split all your money coming in from the little music thing you have going on and miss Nie Nie you will be showing my guys the ins and out of your brilliant scam business, which I'm so very much interested in!"

"So where is my uncle Stacks and where does he stand when it comes to all of this?" "I figured you would ask that. This is all your uncle Stacks idea, I realized just how much of a businessman he was after our little run-in with him early yesterday morning, he tried to resist like any boss would. But my guys flipped him out of his car right into my lap. That's when I gave him the ultimatum to either welcome my supply of uncut product that I can provide for him and force him to cut ties with his connect who just so happened to have his nephew and his girlfriend kidnapped, or say no, and my guys do one last sweep and this time they would not have missed."

"So let me get this right, my uncle found a way to save his ass, all at the same time make a pretty penny along the way?" "Well, Young Reese, that's something you gonna have to ask him yourself." "Yea I feel ya, I have a feeling I already know what he gonna say."

Lil Nie Nie rubs his back then kisses the wound on his forehead then says to her man. "Reese sometimes the truth hurts baby, that's why it's better to go along with THE LIES, WE LIVE WITH."

THE LIES WE LIVE WITH....

WILL BE CONTINUED...

BY: COURTNEY "BLESS" BROWN. © 2023

Made in the USA
Middletown, DE
11 April 2023

28483690R00099